LITTLE JOHN CROW
BY ZIGGY MARLEY & ORLY MARLEY

ILLUSTRATIONS BY GORDON ROWE

Part I
Bull Bay

This is a story about Little John Crow, a young vulture who lived in Bull Bay at the edge of the Blue Mountains on the island of Jamaica in the Caribbean Sea.

From the time he could waddle, before he could even fly, Little John Crow would disobey his parents, ignore their warnings, and find ways to go outside of the cave where they lived to play with his friends.

One bright morning before his parents were up, Little John Crow sneaked outside to be with his best friends: Hummy, the hummingbird, who loved sweets; George, the wise young snake; Missy, the French pigeon; Chiqueen, a feisty chicken hawk; and the Three Little Birds, who sang and did everything together.

After running around and playing games for a while, Little John Crow and his friends were tired, so they sat down near a cool river and had a rest.

While taking turns drinking from the river, they started talking about their parents' jobs and what they wanted to be when they grew up.

"My parents are world travelers, jet-setters really," Missy the pigeon proudly proclaimed in a French accent. "I'm going to be just like them. Voilà!"

"I want to grow up and sssave livesss jussst like my parentsss," George the snake hissed.

"You mean *take* lives," quipped Chiqueen the chicken hawk, who had the smartest mouth in the group.

"Just the sweet nectar of hibiscus for me, just like Mom and Pops," declared Hummy the hummingbird. "It's so yummy!"

"We're already what we want to be," sang the Three Little Birds in a beautiful melody, "the sweetest harmonizing trio in the world."

"Ahhh, who cares," squawked Chiqueen, "I'm just gonna be ME!"

Then it was Little John Crow's turn, but he didn't know what his parents did. You see, Little John Crow was the youngest of his friends, and his parents were waiting for him to be a little older before they explained what they did.

Little John Crow didn't even know what it meant to be a vulture.

"Guys," he said quietly, "I'm too young to know those things."

"You are never too young to think about the future," sang the Three Little Birds, in perfect harmony.

"Thissss issss a great mysssstery," hissed George. "We will help you find out what your parentssss do."

The others agreed with George and joined together to help Little John Crow figure out what his parent did and what great things he would do once he grew up. They all agreed to embark on a quest to find out what Little John Crow's future held in store for him.

The friends left the river and climbed up to the perfect viewing spot—a steep hillside in the Blue Mountains overlooking the cave where Little John Crow and his family lived. There, they could peer down into the valley and see everything that was going on below.

Very quickly, the mystery of Little John Crow's parents' vocation was solved. The friends gasped as they watched two large vultures fly across the sky and swoop down, hunting for food below.

"John's parents aren't r-r-regular birds," stammered Hummy. "They are vu-vu-vultures."

"GROSSSSS, that's not very glamorous, is it?" exclaimed Missy the French pigeon.

"Shhhhhh," said George, who was the first to notice that the two vultures had turned around and were headed straight for them. Scared out of their wits, they all ran away except for Chiqueen, who kept a cautious distance, and Little John Crow.

"Hi Mom, hi Dad," said Little John Crow excitedly.

"What are you doing out of the cave?" asked Mr. Rustle Crow, John's father.

"My friends and I . . ." John started to say. But when he turned around, he found that his friends were nowhere to be seen. Even Chiqueen had quietly slipped away.

"Get back to the cave, son. Mom and I will be back very soon with your breakfast."

And without thinking anything of it, John headed home.

The next day, as soon as his parents had left for work, John once again snuck out and went looking for his friends.

"Hummy! George!" shouted the little vulture, but he couldn't find anyone. Not by the river, not by the big rock shaped like a bull's head, and not by the old mango tree. *Where could they be?* he wondered.

Suddenly, from out of nowhere, Chiqueen appeared. "Hey, Little Johnny, what's *not* cooking?" she joked.

"Where is everyone?" John asked. "Why won't anyone come out and play?"

"You don't know, do you?" Chiqueen responded.

"Know what?"

"The 4-1-1, the intel," Chiqueen said. "This may be news to you, but you're going to be a scavenger, dude! A low-down, dirty, scary, evil vulture. And honestly, I think it's cool."

"Evil? Scary? What do you mean?" John asked. "What do vultures even do?"

"Ohh, they do some nasty stuff, some stinky stuff too," Chiqueen answered. "The only things most vultures eat are dead animals. A vulture's only friend is another vulture, present company excluded of course. *You* don't scare *me*, Little John Crow!"

"Well, what if I don't want to be a vulture? Maybe I can be something else . . . I can be an eagle!" John declared, as he lifted his wings trying to imitate a mighty bald eagle.

"Nope! Still a vulture," said Chiqueen.

"What about a cute, colorful parrot?" John asked, doing his best parrot impersonation.

"Nope! You are still a vulture," insisted Chiqueen.

"What about a peacock?"

"REALLY?!"

"Well, no matter what, I will never, EVER be a scary old *vulture*," said Little John Crow.

After his talk with Chiqueen, John gave up looking for his other friends and headed back to his cave feeling very sad. He was afraid he would never get to play with them again.

"What's wrong, Little John?" asked his mom, Mrs. Sharil Crow, when she saw the expression on his face.

"My friends don't want to play with me anymore because I'm going to be a scary, stinky, evil vulture like you and Daddy, and I don't want to be a vulture, Mom." Tears ran down Little John Crow's face.

"John Crow, listen to me and listen well—you are a vulture and you should be proud of who you are," Mrs. Sharil Crow explained. "We are all here for a purpose, we are all connected, we are all important. Even vultures. Your friends will accept you for who you are as long as you accept yourself first. Besides, we don't eat *living* animals, only dead ones."

The next morning, Little John Crow stayed in the cave while his parents went off to work, flying a few miles away to where Farmer Badson lived with his wife Evelin and their daughter Darling.

Farmer Badson was up early, feeding his farm animals, when he noticed that his prized goat, Jolly, was missing.

Farmer Badson immediately went off in search of Jolly. He didn't have to look long before he came upon a scene that made him very unhappy.

Little John Crow's parents were doing exactly what vultures are supposed to do, but Farmer Badson didn't see it that way. He'd lost his favorite goat and he blamed Little John Crow's parents. What he did next was extremely upsetting.

Back in the mountains, the animals could hear the sounds of a struggle echoing in the distance. Chiqueen, who was standing by the old mango tree with George, Hummy, and Missy, decided to see what was going on for herself.

"I'll be right back," she said as she flew off. And almost as quickly as Chiqueen had taken off, she returned.

Little John Crow had also heard the commotion and knew something wasn't right, so he ran from his cave to the mango tree where his friends usually played. When he got there he saw that everyone was talking all at once.

"What's going on, guys?" asked the little vulture.

Everyone except Chiqueen turned around and slowly walked away without saying a word.

Chiqueen flew over and landed next to John.

"Sad news, Buzzy. Your parents, well . . . they are gone. Farmer Badson did a very terrible thing. I'm sorry, Little John Crow, but you might never see them again."

"Why?!" asked John.

"Nobody likes vultures, Buzzy. It's just a fact of life. These days, even bloodsucking vampires are more popular around here than vultures."

"WHAT??" exclaimed John.

"Ahh forget it," said Chiqueen. "Just be careful, Johnny Boy. I wouldn't want what happened to your parents to happen to *you*."

Feeling unloved, alone, and unwanted, Little John Crow quietly decided to leave the hills of Bull Bay and the only home he'd ever known, promising to himself to never return.

"Where are you going?" asked Chiqueen as she watched her friend head off.

"Nowhere," answered John as he disappeared into the shadows.

Part II

The Kettle

For days on end, Little John Crow wandered aimlessly through the Blue Mountains. He was completely alone, but he staggered on, hungry and tired. Sometimes he would fly a few feet before crashing to the ground with exhaustion.

After one such crash landing, Little John Crow lifted his head up and caught sight of three figures in the distance. Using his very last bit of energy, he hurried to catch up to them.

"Excuse me, excuse me," John said once he got close enough for them to hear his cries. And while he stopped to catch his breath, he began to make out what they were—vultures!

Remembering that vultures were mean and scary, John started to move away, but he was quickly cornered by the three of them.

"Well, well, well, what do we have here so?" said Rude Bwoy, the skinniest of the group.

"Hey, dis our turf, kiddo. Get lost, *capuhy*!" said Bubbler, an overweight vulture who was trying his best to sound like a tough guy he had once seen on TV.

"How many times do I have to tell you it's *capisce*, you birdbrain!" said Pat, who was clearly the leader of these vultures. Then, turning to Little John Crow, she said, "What do you want? Can't you see we're busy?"

John tried to answer: "I . . . I . . ." But he was so tired and filled with fear that he fainted before he could say another word.

When Little John Crow woke up, he was in a dark cave—a much nicer one than the cave he and his parents lived in.

"Where am I?" he asked. "Are you going to, you know, do the vulture thing?"

"Do the vulture t'ing?" laughed Rude Bwoy. "Of course we going to do the vulture t'ing. We are vultures, dat what we do."

"Here you go, kiddo," said Bubbler, offering John something to eat. "Have some grub. You look starved."

"You're not going to eat me?" said John.

"I don't know what you've heard about us," answered Pat, "but we don't just go around eating everything we happen to come upon."

"Especially if it's still walking around," said Bubbler.

"Right, right," added Rude Boy as he fist-bumped Bubbler.

"What's your story, anyway?" asked Pat. "A young buzzard like yourself isn't usually wandering around all alone."

So Little John Crow told his story, explaining how he ended up in his current situation. "Vultures don't have any friends," he concluded.

"Hey, little chick, we have friends—look at us. We three, we are besties," proclaimed Rude Bwoy.

"But you're all vultures," said John.

"Duh! Of course we are, that's how we roll it," said Bubbler.

"*Roll*, that's how we *roll* is what he means," said Pat.

"I think I get where this turkey is coming from," said Bubbler. "Yeah, he wants to be friends with all types of animals and maybe even humans."

"You *so* innocent, little chick," Rude Bwoy said as he patted the little vulture's head.

"Not sure about the *humans* part," replied Little John Crow.

"Humans? Now *that's* a scary, mean bunch if ever I saw one!" declared Rude Bwoy. "But *we* get the bad reputation?!"

Several moments later Bubbler asked, "Are we having turkey for dinner?"

"Hey, I didn't get your name," said Pat.

"It's John."

"John, you can get along with anyone if they are truly your friends," said Pat, "and accept you for who you are."

"Yeah," said Bubbler, "and we vultures have to love who we are no matter what those other birdbrains say."

"Cats are nice," said Rudy Bwoy. "Fuzzy, cuddly . . ."

"Alright, alright . . . meet up," announced Pat, and the three vultures gathered together and continued to talk quietly as Little John Crow looked on.

"Okay then," Pat said, turning to face Little John Crow. "We have decided to make you a member of our kettle."

"Kettle?" said John, a note of confusion in his voice.

"Yeah, it's what we call a group of vultures," explained Rude Bwoy. "It's vulture culture."

"John, welcome to the Committee," said Bubbler.

"What does *that* mean?" asked John.

"It means we are going to bestow upon you the ancient secrets of all Vulture Committees," replied Pat.

"We going to teach you how to be a true vulture brotha," said Rude Bwoy.

"Yeah, we start tomorrow after porridge," said Bubbler.

"After forage—he means after *forage*," said Pat. "Now get some rest! You are definitely going to need it."

The next afternoon, following a morning of foraging, Pat, Rude Bwoy, and Bubbler sat Little John Crow down in a big ackee tree and began schooling him on the ancient secrets of the Committee, beginning with the true name of vultures.

"We weren't always reviled by others. In fact, far back in time we were known as *Cathartes aura*, which means Golden Purifier, and we were given special treatment."

"Yeah. Without us, the world would be a mess. Literally," said Bubbler, rubbing his full tummy.

"Everyone and everything have its worth, mon," said Rude Bwoy.

"You see, John," Pat went on, "we have a long history going back to ancient Egypt where we adorned the headdresses of royalty. We were respected and loved. Not everyone saw us as creepy—many saw us as sacred creatures. Some still do."

"Yup!" Bubbler chimed in. "And we also have a great sense of smell and excellent eyesight, which is very useful in our line of work, if you know what I mean, brotha."

"We even have our own holiday," said Rude Bwoy. "It's called Every-day, mon." Pat and Bubbler broke out into laughter.

Pat, Bubbler, and Rude Bwoy continued to teach John about vulture culture. Over the next few months, he grew bigger and stronger and even figured out how to fly.

With the help of his new friends, John began to learn how to love and accept himself. Being a vulture was actually a very important job . . . not to mention, kinda cool . . .

Every so often, while he was flying around with Pat, Bubbler, and Rude Bwoy, John would think about what his mother said to him: "We are all here for a purpose, we are all connected, we are all important."

Part III

A State of Grace

Back in the Blue Mountains, however, life was not going so well. There had been a terrible stench in the air for a very long time, and it was becoming unbearable. Without the vulture family around, things weren't quite right.

George, the wise old snake, called for a meeting and animals came from everywhere to take part.

"The ssssituation issss bad," said George. "We musssst take action!"

"Hey, Mr. Brainiac, tell us something we don't know," grumbled Chiqueen.

"Excuse my French, but *arrivez à point*," said Missy.

"As long as it involves something sweet, I'm all for it," said Hummy.

"We need to find Little John Crow," said George. "I have a feeling he and hisss family have sssomething to do with our sssituation."

"Of course they do! Don't you *all* see that?" exclaimed Chiqueen. "Whatever is happening here started not long after we stopped seeing John and his family around here. We should have treated John as a friend and not judged him because of who he is or who his parents are. Who cares if he's a vulture? Who cares if I'm a chicken hawk?"

"Ahem, you mean besides chickens of course," giggled Hummy.

"What do vultures even have to do with all this mess we're in?" asked Missy.

"A lot, I think," said George.

"*Monsieur*, we don't need vulturrrez to fix our problemz," said Missy in her snooty tone.

"Excuse me, wise snake, sir," Chiqueen said with a smirk on her face, "I have a question. How exactly are pigeons who speak French helpful in this situation?"

"Everyone pleassse jussst calm down," said George. "If we are to sssolve thisss ssstench, we mussst work together. Pleassse, everyone, do your bessst to find out where Little John Crow could have gone. The sssooner the better! Whether we believe it or not, we need him . . ."

So all the animals went off to find Little John Crow, using their various skills—Missy used her pigeon connections to hone in on his last-seen location; Hummy checked in with his friends in the hibiscus network; Chiqueen flew high above trying to spot anything that would give her a clue as to where John might be.

After nearly a week of searching, Chiqueen, Missy, and Hummy returned to share the information they had gathered.

"According to what you have all sssaid and my calculationsss," began George, "our friend headed in the direction of Bone Valley—the mossst lifelesss, ssscary, sssomber, desssolate place you never want to go. I don't expect any of us could sssurvive out there. No one should ever go to Bone Valley."

"I will!" shouted Chiqueen. "I'll go to Bone Valley!"

"Fais bon voyage!" called out Missy as she watched the chicken hawk fly away.

Chiqueen didn't even glance back at her friends. There was no doubt in her mind that only Little John Crow could fix their problems, so she traveled through the day and into the night, barely stopping in her search for her friend.

John Crow, who was no longer so little, had fully embraced vulture culture. As he grew and flourished, he had transformed from being timid and unsure of himself into a beautiful, majestic creature. The others now looked up to him, imagining that he might one day become the new king vulture. John even wrote a song about it:

"I'm a vulture / you're a vulture / be a vulture true. / Do your duty / it might be dirty / but that is what we do. / Take a whirl, clean the world / sometimes make a little stew. / I'm a vulture / you're a vulture / be a vulture true."

"That's my joint!" proclaimed Bubbler.

"Positive vibes, mon," added Rude Bwoy.

"I hate to break up the jam session," said Pat, who was always on guard, "but my keen vulture senses are telling me that we may have a little job to do."

"Let's go!" said John as he took to the air. "This is what we dooo . . ."

Pat, Rude Bwoy, and Bubbler followed John Crow's lead. They formed a kettle and soon started circling a small figure stumbling below them.

"What is it?" asked John.

"By my keen sight, I would say in a little while it will be lunch," answered Bubbler.

"Can you go down there and take a closer look?" asked John.

"Yes sir," the three vultures answered as they descended.

Bubbler landed just ahead of the stumbling figure. "Yo, yo, you there! No offense, but how long before, you know . . . you croak? We're on a strict union time frame here."

"Buzz . . . off," replied the weary traveler, falling down onto the parched ground. Bone Valley was not a hospitable place if you weren't a vulture.

Pat and Rude Bwoy landed a few feet behind.

"Is it lunchtime?" asked Pat.

"Not yet. But how 'bout we help you along," Bubbler said, turning toward the traveler on the ground. "You know, end the misery and all that."

As the vultures began to approach, John Crow swooped down and announced, "Me first," heading straight toward the helpless figure.

But just as John Crow was about to strike, he suddenly hesitated, looking surprised and confused. His instinct said one thing, but his heart said another.

"I was afraid he wasn't king material," whispered Rude Bwoy, as he slowly moved toward John and the traveler on the ground.

"Stop!" commanded John, and with a strong flap of his wing, Rude Bwoy was pushed back. "I know who this is. This is one of my friends. Chiqueen, can you hear me?"

"Little John, is that you?" mumbled the chicken hawk. "It sounds like you, but you look . . . different."

"Does this mean we're not having lunch?" asked Bubbler.

"Stop it, you birdbrain!" snapped Pat. "Do you want the people reading this book to think we don't have a heart? We may be vultures but we still have rules, and there are certain things we won't do despite what you may have heard."

"You talking to me?" said Bubbler.

"NO! I'm talking to *them*," replied Pat sarcastically.

"Them *who*?" asked Rude Bwoy.

"Never mind," said Pat. "Let's just all go back to our cave."

After a little rest and some nourishment, Chiqueen was herself again. She couldn't believe what she was seeing. The little vulture she'd known was no more. Instead, John was this great, magnificent creature.

She told the Committee what had been happening ever since the vultures left the Blue Mountains, and how she'd been sent to find Little John Crow and ask him to come back, for without him they were doomed.

But John Crow was unsure of how to react to this request. He was enjoying his time in Bone Valley so much. And it was hard for him to imagine going back to a place where there were so many memories of his parents, and where his kind were looked down on. Still, something inside of him wanted to help.

After carefully considering Chiqueen's request, he proclaimed, "I'll do it!"

"You might be biting off a likkle more dan what you can chew," said Rude Bwoy, rubbing his tummy.

"Don't worry. If I need you guys, I'll send a signal."

So, with Chiqueen fully recovered, John said goodbye to his friends and the two of them flew off toward the Blue Mountains to save Bull Bay.

As John Crow and Chiqueen descended into the Blue Mountains, the vulture could not believe what he was seeing. The land that was once full of laughter and joy—his playground as a young buzzard—was now a gloomy place, and there was a terrible stench that only a vulture could love.

John knew what he needed to do: he sent the signal to get help from his vulture buddies.

As soon as Bubbler, Rude Bwoy, and Pat arrived, they formed a kettle in the sky above Bull Bay to scope out the buffet.

"Boys and girl, let's feast!" declared John Crow.

With determination in their eyes and the wind beneath their wings, John, Rude Bwoy, Pat, and Bubbler swooped down like a rainbow. By day's end they had magically brought the Blue Mountains back to a state of harmony.

"Yay!" shouted all of John's friends who hadn't seen him in a long time.

"Welcome home," sang the Three Little Birds.

"It'sss nice to sssee you," said George.

"*Merci bookoo*," said Missy.

But just as they all gathered around the old mango tree to celebrate, Farmer Badson appeared. The tension in the air could be felt by everyone.

"Uh-oh, it's about to get not very nice," lamented Chiqueen.

John Crow angrily leaped toward Farmer Badson, but he saw something he couldn't believe that stopped him in his tracks: his parents soaring through the sky toward the mango tree.

John was so overcome with joy that he immediately forgot about the farmer. He met his parents at the base of the tree and hugged them with all his strength.

Farmer Badson apologized for his past behavior. He explained that he'd misunderstood the importance of every individual creature and promised never to mistreat another animal ever again.

When his land had filled with the terrible stench, he realized his mistake and had gone off in search of John's parents—who'd managed to escape from him and had flown to another valley to hide.

John's parents explained that they had never stopped looking for him this whole time, and they were jubilant to find him alive and healthy.

Bull Bay and the Blue Mountains were restored to their natural state. The ecosystem was balanced once more.

The Three Little Birds sang their favorite song and everyone danced and celebrated.

Words and story by Ziggy Marley & Orly Marley
Illustrations by Gordon Rowe
Executive produced by Tuff Gong Worldwide

©2021 Tuff Gong Worldwide, LLC
Published by Akashic Books/Tuff Gong Worldwide Books
ISBN: 978-1-61775-980-2
Library of Congress Control Number: 2021935237

First printing
Printed in China

Akashic Books
Brooklyn, New York
Twitter: @AkashicBooks
Facebook: AkashicBooks
E-mail: info@akashicbooks.com
Website: www.akashicbooks.com

Orly Marley and Ziggy Marley

ZIGGY MARLEY is an eight-time GRAMMY Award winner, Emmy Award winner, author, philanthropist, and reggae icon. He has released thirteen albums to much critical acclaim, and is the author of three other children's books: *I Love You Too*, *Music Is in Everything*, and *My Dog Romeo*; as well the *Ziggy Marley and Family Cookbook*. His album *Family Time* scored a GRAMMY Award for Best Children's Album and his latest children's album, *More Family Time*, was released in September 2020 via Tuff Gong Worldwide.

ORLY MARLEY is an Israeli-born entrepreneur and music manager. After a thirteen-year career at the William Morris Agency, she became the president of Tuff Gong Worldwide and Ishti Music. Together with Ziggy, she heads Unlimited Resources Giving Enlightenment (U.R.G.E.), a nonprofit organization that seeks to make enduring contributions to the lives of children in Jamaica, Africa, and throughout the world.

GORDON ROWE is a Toronto-born illustrator and designer working in digital painting, acrylic painting, gouache painting, and portraiture. He illustrates and art directs for album artwork and editorials, and has worked with several high-profile clients in the music industry.

Photo by Ricky Viray

Also available from Ziggy Marley

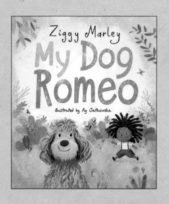

MY DOG ROMEO by Ziggy Marley
Illustrations by Ag Jatkowska
A children's picture book

Ziggy Marley's ode to his four-legged friend Romeo becomes a picture book that is sure to touch the hearts of dog lovers everywhere.

MUSIC IS IN EVERYTHING by Ziggy Marley
Illustrations by Ag Jatkowska
A children's picture book

A picture book based on Ziggy Marley's popular song celebrating music's many forms, from the sounds of ocean waves to laughter in the family kitchen.

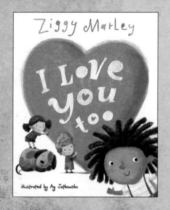

I LOVE YOU TOO by Ziggy Marley
Illustrations by Ag Jatkowska
A children's picture book

"Sure to be a hit at bedtime, the lyrical story conveys the sweet, soothing, and affirming message."
—*School Library Journal*

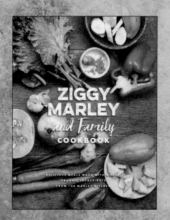

ZIGGY MARLEY AND FAMILY COOKBOOK

"[Ziggy's] first collection of recipes pays homage to the flavors of his youth and the food he loves to cook for his wife and five children." —*People*

"With a health-focused approach, Ziggy Marley reveals memories and food traditions in his new family cookbook." —*Ebony*